THE LOST LIBRARY

JESS McGEACHIN

VIKING

When Oliver moved to a new house,
he had to leave lots of things behind.

But at least he had his books. He could escape
to different worlds with the turn of a page.

Oliver knew all about books,
but even he was surprised
to find one fluttering behind
his bedroom closet.

It must have been left behind, thought Oliver.

He would have loved to keep it . . .

Please return to:
THE
LOST
LIBRARY

but it belonged
somewhere else.

Where was the Lost Library?
Surely someone must know,
thought Oliver.

But everyone was too busy . . .

or too sleepy to pay
any attention.

Everyone except for Rosie,
his new neighbor.

"I know someone who might be able to help,"
she said with a smile.

Oliver and Rosie walked quietly to the front desk.

The fluttering book closed its covers
and dropped into Oliver's hand.

"We can ask the librarian," said Rosie.

But Oliver had a better idea.
He gently slipped the book into the returns slot.

No sooner had it disappeared than the floor beneath them gave way.

They hurtled down . . .

and down . . .

and down.

They landed with
a soft *thud*.

Books of every shape
and size filled the
shelves around them.

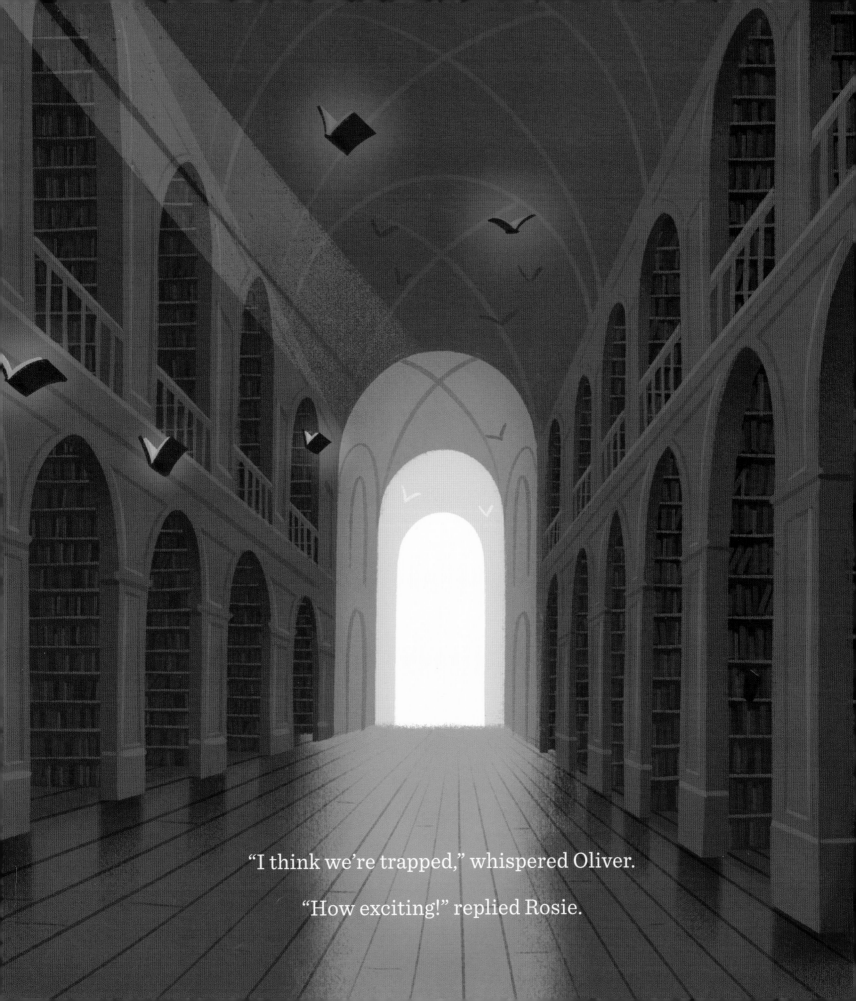

"I think we're trapped," whispered Oliver.

"How exciting!" replied Rosie.

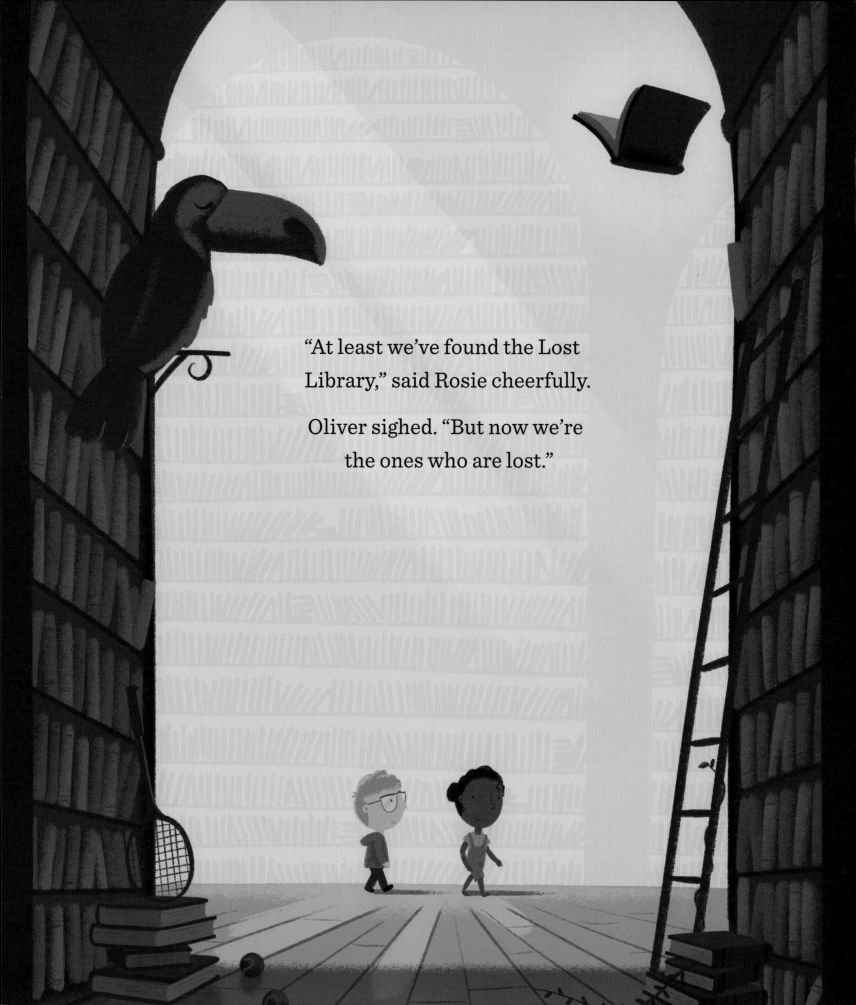

"At least we've found the Lost Library," said Rosie cheerfully.

Oliver sighed. "But now we're the ones who are lost."

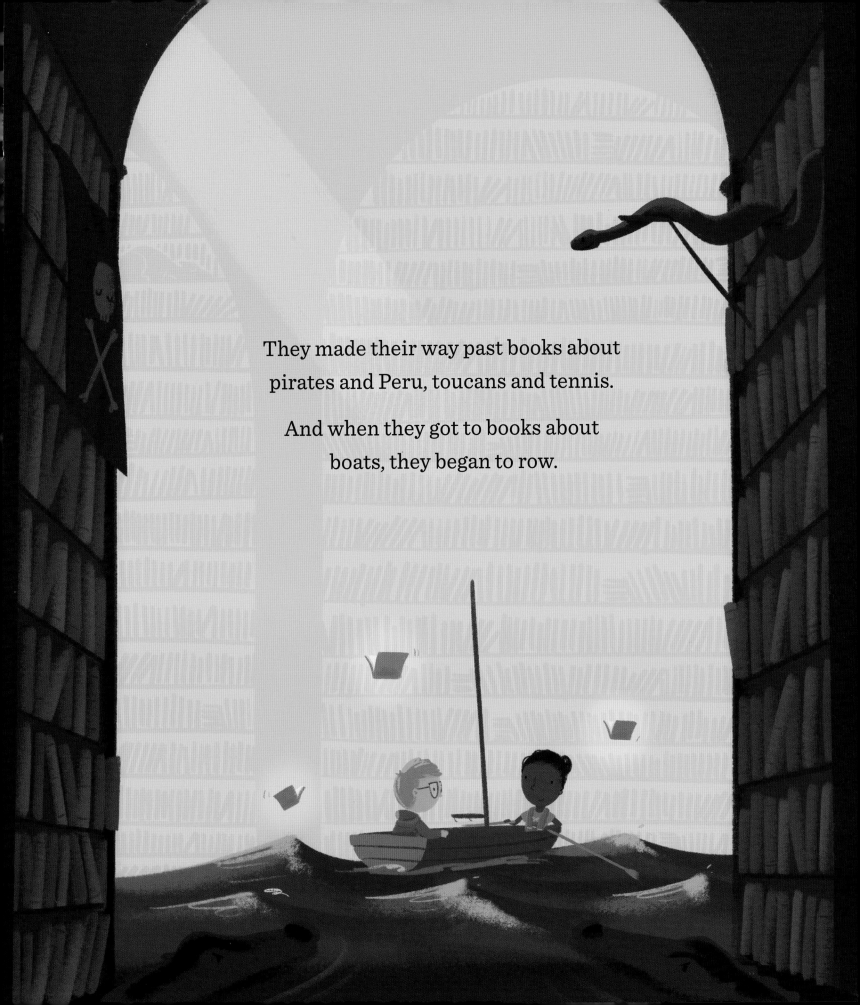

They made their way past books about
pirates and Peru, toucans and tennis.

And when they got to books about
boats, they began to row.

As they sailed past books about storms, Oliver felt nervous. "I'm not a very good swimmer," he said, but his words were lost to the wind.

Luckily, just within reach,
Rosie found a book to help.

Oliver read how to knot
a bowline and hoist
the mainsail . . .

and Rosie sailed them
safely to shore.

As they walked, they
found themselves
surrounded by trees.

Just a few at first,
then more and more
until a forest of books
towered above.

"Let's go right," said Rosie.

"I think left," replied Oliver.

But in the end it didn't matter—
there was no path to follow.

"We'll never find our way out," Oliver said.

But, just as he was losing hope, Rosie found another book to help.

"We need to stay calm and stick together," she said.

Slowly the forest began to thin.

And there, at last, at the top of
a tall bookshelf, Oliver spied
the way out.

But the bookshelf had spied them too!

For this was no ordinary bookshelf—
this was a Bookshelf Dragon.

"Watch out, Oliver!"
called Rosie.

The dragon snapped and snarled.
It didn't like being woken up at all.

Oliver was sure he was
about to be eaten, and
there was no book to
help with that.

But there was a Rosie.

For Rosie had calmly
sat down and begun
to read aloud . . .

If there's one thing
everyone likes, it's
being read to.

Slowly, the Bookshelf Dragon
drifted off to sleep.

Oliver and Rosie climbed quietly up the
dragon's back, careful not to wake it.

As they passed the librarian, Oliver paused.

"Excuse me. Have you ever heard of a Bookshelf Dragon?" he asked.

Ms. Hardback gave him a knowing smile. "That's a story for another day."

Oliver and Rosie loved reading together. They could visit different worlds with the turn of a page.

And they always kept an eye out for lost books . . .

Just in case.

For Mum, and for librarians—keepers of the magic.

Dear Reader,
Ever bold and sage.
Can you find a dragon
Before you turn each page?

MS. Hardback

VIKING

An imprint of Penguin Random House LLC, New York

First published in the United States of America by Viking,
an imprint of Penguin Random House LLC, 2022

First published in Australia by Puffin Books, an imprint of Penguin Random House Australia Pty Ltd, 2020

Philomel Books is a registered trademark of Penguin Random House LLC.

Visit us online at penguinrandomhouse.com.

Library of Congress Cataloging-in-Publication Data is available.

ISBN 9780593351338

Manufactured in China

1 3 5 7 9 10 8 6 4 2

TOPL

US edition edited by Liza Kaplan.
US edition designed by Monique Sterling.
Text set in Sabon.